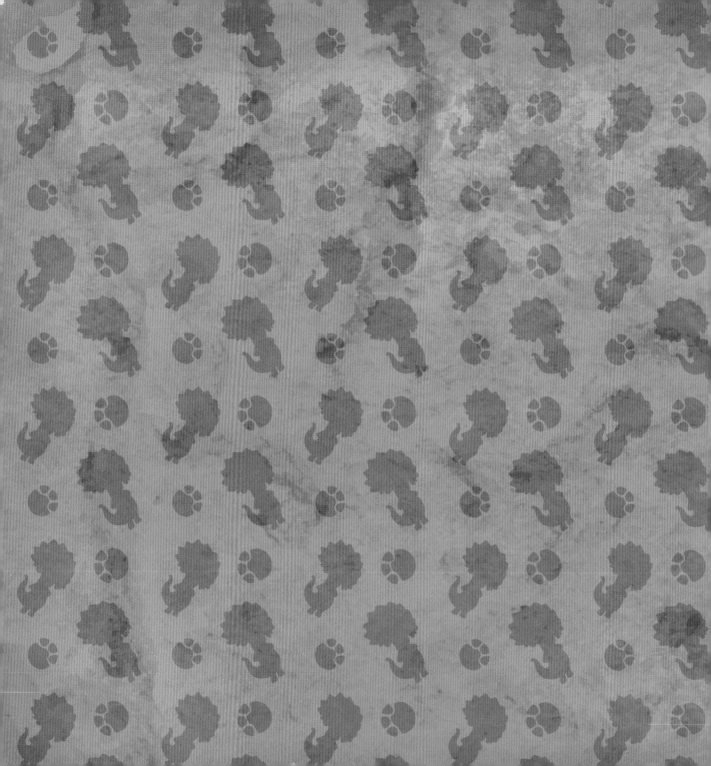

GIGANTOSAURUS™

Try Again, TINY

CANDLEWICK
ENTERTAINMENT

First U.S. edition 2020
First published by Templar Books, an imprint of Bonnier Books UK 2020

Library of Congress Catalog Card Number pending
ISBN 978-1-5362-1409-3

20 21 22 23 24 25 TWP 10 9 8 7 6 5 4 3 2 1

Printed in Johor Bahru, Malaysia

This book was typeset in Kosmik BoldOne and Kosmik PlainTwo.
The illustrations were created digitally.

Candlewick Entertainment
an imprint of
Candlewick Press
99 Dover Street
Somerville, Massachusetts 02144

visit us at www.candlewick.com

Tiny's favorite flower is
hidden in these pages.

How many can you find?

This story is all about **TINY**, the little triceratops who knows how to have fun. Tiny loves dancing, singing, and telling jokes. So when it's time for her very important dino test, it's hard for her to take it seriously! Will Tiny have to change her fun-loving ways to fit in with the rest of the triceratops herd?

The four dino friends were busy with one of their favorite activities — spying on Giganto! Rocky stood on Mazu, who stood on Bill, who stood on Tiny. She might be the smallest, but Tiny was one STRONG dinosaur!

Suddenly, the tower of dinos began to wobble dangerously. Was it an earthquake? Or, worse, a GROUNDWOBBLER?

No, it was Tiny, performing some of *her* favorite activities ... singing and dancing!

Hey, careful down there!

It's not me, it's Tiny!

Bill must be moving!

Oh, life is *FUN* and *FUN* is *TOPS* when *you're* a *TRI-CERA-TOPS!*

"This is not the time to mess around, Tiny! Giganto will hear us!" Mazu hissed.

Sure enough, the mighty dinosaur took a giant STOMP toward them, and their shaky tower tumbled to the ground.

The friends landed in a heap right in front of Tiny's big brother, Trey.

Trey chuckled as he helped the four little dinos to their feet. "I'm glad I bumped into you, Sis. I've been looking all over Cretacea for you!"

Tiny explained that they had been hiding from Giganto. Trey looked at Tiny.

You're a TRICERATOPS!

"YOU don't need to hide from anyone," he told her.
"We triceratops are a brave and strong herd of WARRIORS!"

Tiny wasn't so sure. "I'm actually a better dancer than warrior," she said.
She did a little dance to show her brother what she could do. Trey just laughed.

Look at my awesome moves!

It was time for Trey to teach Tiny all the skills she needed to learn.
"We need to prepare for your TRICERATOPS TRIAL," he said.

"Every triceratops has to complete this special test to prove their strength to the herd," said Trey. "First, the DEAD TREE TACKLE."

Trey used his powerful horns to uproot a big old tree. It fell to the ground with a CRASH.

"How about YOU tackle the tree and then I DECORATE it?" suggested Tiny.

Let's make it look pretty!

Tiny loved to draw and decorate
almost as much as she loved dancing!

"Very funny, Sis," replied Trey.

But for once, Tiny wasn't joking!

"Next, we do the STOMPS," said Trey. He jumped UP . . . and landed with a mighty
THUMP that sent the smaller dinos flying into the air! They all giggled as they
bounced up and down.

Then it was Tiny's turn. She tried to stomp just like Trey had showed her.

But it wasn't long before Tiny had turned the moves into a break dance! Her friends cheered as she hopped, bopped, and swung her tail before finishing with a head spin.

Trey was not impressed.

Next it was time for the TRICERATOPS TUG. "Grab my horn and see if you can get me to budge," Trey instructed Tiny.

Trey was so BIG and HEAVY! Tiny had an idea. She jumped on Trey's back and began to sing, but Trey stopped her before she could finish.

Tiny DID want to take the trial seriously, but she couldn't help turning it into something fun.

Tree tackle and toss, then tug and stomp.
The Triceratops Trial — what a romp!

"Triceratops are STRONG. We like to push BIG things around. And we are VERY SERIOUS about it!" Trey said.

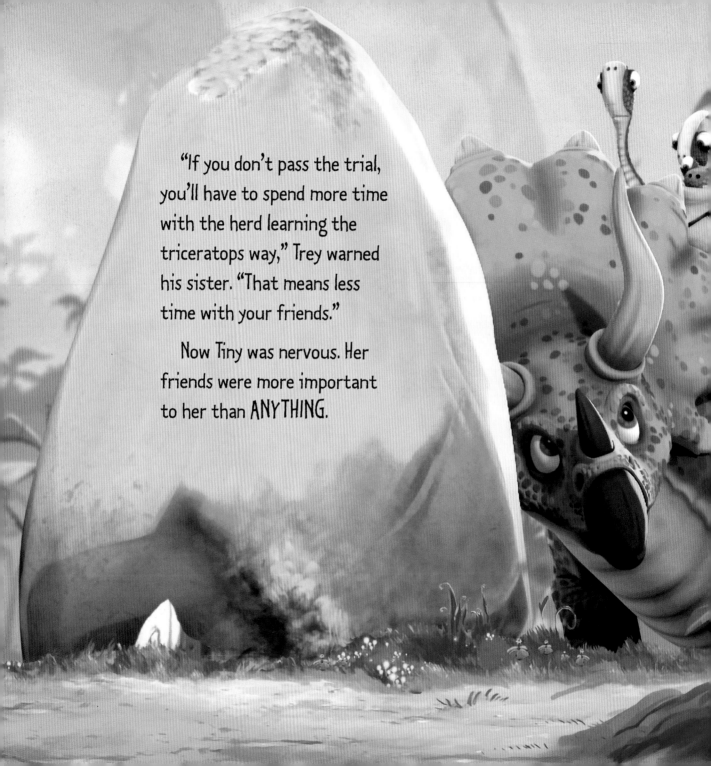

"If you don't pass the trial, you'll have to spend more time with the herd learning the triceratops way," Trey warned his sister. "That means less time with your friends."

Now Tiny was nervous. Her friends were more important to her than ANYTHING.

Then it was time for Trey to teach Tiny the TREE TOSS. But instead of throwing the tree, Tiny wedged one end under Trey's foot and used it as a catapult to fling HERSELF into the air.

"Look who's flying now!" Tiny shouted as she sailed through the air and then landed in front of her brother.

"That's enough!" Trey said. "If you don't get serious, you'll never pass the Triceratops Trial!"

"Sorry, Trey," said Tiny. "I do WANT to be a good triceratops, but I like doing things my own way."

There's only one way to do things — the RIGHT way!

Suddenly there was a loud ROAR behind them . . .

GIGANTOSAURUS!

All the commotion had disturbed Giganto, and he did NOT look happy! He came thundering toward the dinosaurs.

RUUUUN!

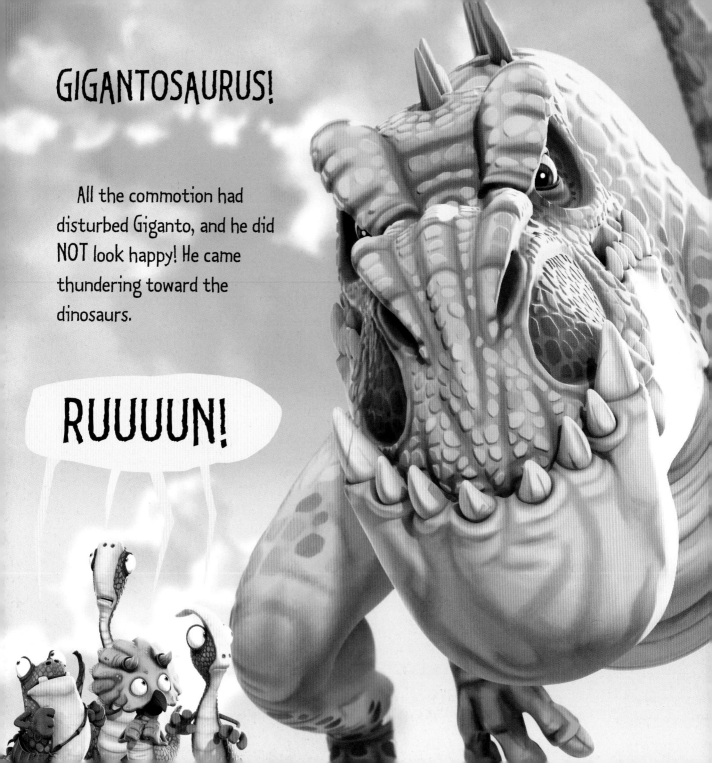

Tiny, Rocky, Mazu, and Bill raced through the jungle until Giganto's STOMPS were well behind them. THEY were safe, but they'd lost Trey! They retraced their steps and found him stuck in quicksand — and he was sinking!

Tiny tried to TUG Trey out, but it was no use. Then she had another idea. Tiny TACKLED a tree to the ground and TOSSED it next to her brother.

Nicely done, little sis!

The four little dinosaurs slid the tree trunk underneath Trey and jumped onto one end. Trey was catapulted out of the quicksand. It worked just like the tree catapult that Tiny made earlier!

"Looks like you learned a thing or two after all," said Trey. At last, he was back on solid ground. "You did it!" He smiled at Tiny. "And you did it YOUR way."

Can you get off us now?

Later that day, Trey gathered the herd together. It was time to watch Tiny's Triceratops Trial. They waited silently for it to begin.

"Welcome, fellow triceratops warriors! My sister Tiny is one of the bravest in all Cretacea," Trey said proudly. "She's clever enough to get me out of quicksand, and she performs our trial tasks like no one else!"

Trey turned to his sister, who was looking anxious.
He wished her luck — but he knew she didn't really need it!

Tiny took a deep breath and stepped out in front of the herd.
It was showtime! Would all her practice pay off?

First, Tiny fiercely
TACKLED and TOSSED a tree.

Then she showed her strength
in STOMPING and TUGGING.

Of course, she completed each
task in her own special Tiny way!

When she finished, there was a LONG pause . . . before the triceratops herd began to stomp their feet in approval.

Tiny had passed! There was only one way to celebrate — with a dance, of course. And this time, even Trey joined in!

That was how Tiny learned that she didn't have to change to get the approval of her herd. She proved that being true to yourself is the best way to be! Tiny even found that she **CAN** be serious sometimes . . . serious about having fun, that is!

What does a triceratops sit on?
Its tricera-bottom!

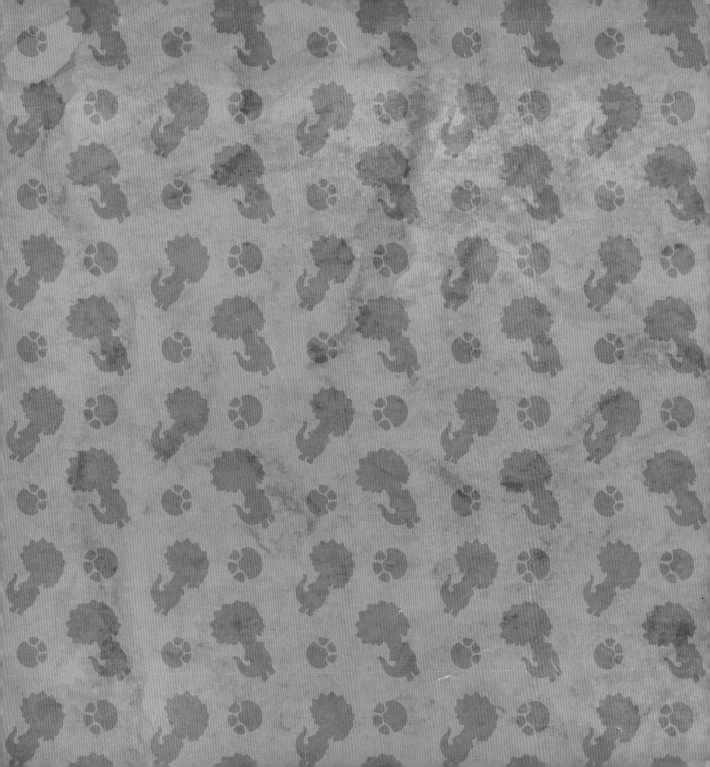

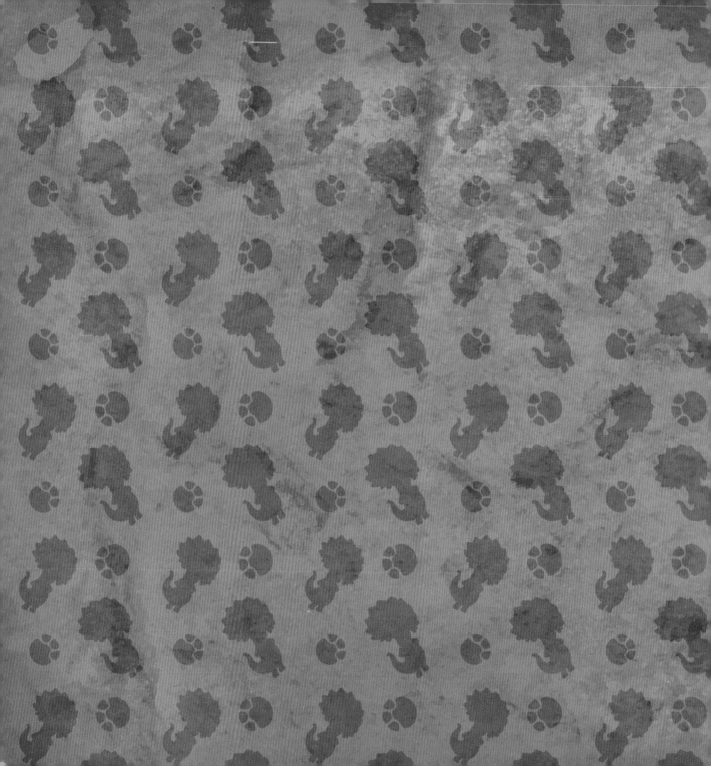